SUPER SAN

SIMON & SCHUSTER BOOKS
FOR YOUNG READERS
Simon & Schuster Building
Rockefeller Center
1230 Avenue of the Americas
New York, New York 10020
Text copyright © 1991 by Annie
Civardi. Illustrations copyright ©
1991 by Clive Scruton

PERCY PENGUIN TO UNCOVER THE SECRETS OF SANTA

Never before in the history of Icy Land has a penguin visited the North Pole. But, late last night, from his throne in Iceberg Castle, the Emperor Penguin made an announcement.

A letter has arrived from Santa inviting Percy Penguin, our chief reporter, to Santa City.

Percy will be the first penguin to visit the North Pole, and the lucky reporter chosen to divulge Santa's secrets to the world.

Every week until Christmas, Percy will send us back a Super Santa Story.

Good luck, Percy Penguin!

**Library of Congress
Cataloging-in-Publication
Data**
Civardi, Annie
The secrets of Santa / by Annie
Civardi : illustrated by Clive
Scruton.
Summary: In a series of
newspaper articles, Percy Penguin
reporter for the South Polar
Times, describes his trip to Santa
City.
[1. Santa Claus—Fiction. 2.
Christmas—Fiction. 3.
Reporters and reporting—Fiction
I. Scruton, Clive, ill. II. Tit
[E]—dc20   91-1
ISBN 0-671-74270-1

Manufactured in Singapore

THE SECRETS OF

SANTA

By Percy Penguin as told to

ANNIE CIVARDI

Illustrated by

CLIVE SCRUTON

For Todd, Sophie, Jake and Amber
A. C.

For Ben and Hannah's Grandpa, with love
C. S.

Simon & Schuster
Books for Young Readers
Published by Simon & Schuster
New York • London • Toronto
Sydney • Tokyo • Singapore

I'm Percy Penguin, chief reporter for the South Polar Times. As you've probably read, I'm about to go to Santa City. Imagine Santa choosing *me* to tell the world his secrets. What a fantastic scoop!

I say goodbye to the Emperor Penguin and promise not to leave a snowball unturned until I find out *everything* there is to know about Santa.

My bags are packed and I'm ready to go. I've got everything a good reporter needs — my trusty old tape recorder, my note pad and my camera.

It's a long way to Santa City...

through the steamy jungle...

over high mountain peaks...

across the burning desert...

and around crowded cities.

At last I arrive!

As soon as I arrive at the North Pole, Sid the Snowman drives me straight to Santa City.

Santa lives in a glistening white palace with his assistant, a polar bear called Gloria, and six little elves — Robin, Holly, Ivy, Carol, Snowflake and Noel.

One of the elves lets me in. Ooops! I seem to be a bit early. Santa's still in bed having his breakfast.

I can hardly believe it's really Santa. He's just as jolly and rosy and round as I'd always imagined. Just think! I'm about to meet him and discover all his secrets.

Santa stops at the Ice Port on his way to the Santa City Post Office. What a noisy place!

All night long, his special delivery planes have been landing on the runway. They're packed with letters from children.

Lots of big, strong snowmen hurry to unload the huge sacks of mail.

Flapping flippers! There's another plane circling around the Ice Port. Poor Santa will have a lot of reading to do today.

This must be the busiest post office in the world. The elves in the sorting room open the letters for Santa to read. Whopping whales! What a job! Icy Land doesn't get this many letters in a whole year.

After Santa has read all the letters and made all the toys the children want this year, the snowmen file them in a special room. Santa never *ever* throws a single letter away.

Santa finishes reading today's batch of mail. A little girl has asked him for a flying penguin. Can you believe it? She wants a toy like me.

Now we're in Santa's Playroom. Santa checks his penguin cupboard. Nope, he hasn't got any *flying* penguins. He'll have to invent one.

Frozen fishcakes! Santa's so clever. His Playroom's full of toys he's already invented. I'm sure it won't take him long to make a flying penguin.

Santa works hard on his flying penguin until it's absolutely perfect. Then he lets me in on one of his biggest secrets.

Guess what? Santa has his own special top secret toy factory right in the middle of Santa City! Absolutely nobody's allowed in here without permission.

I can't believe my eyes! This must be the most exciting place in the whole wide world. There are gigantic toy machines everywhere. Hundreds of elves and snowmen are hard at work, testing and checking, then loading the toys to take to Santa's warehouse. There's even a machine to wrap them up.

Flapping flippers! What's that over there? It's an enormous penguin machine and it's making hundreds of baby flying penguins. I'll have to take a photograph to go with my first Super Santa Story in the South Polar Times.

First the snowmen drop the penguin parts into the top of the machine. Let's take a closer look.

Help!

Oh no, now I'm a flying penguin.

I'm all wrapped up!

Hey you, put me down.

Phew, I'm free at last.

Next I meet Santa and Gloria at Fred's Sew and Sew Shop. Fred's the finest tailor in Santa City. Every year, he makes Santa a new suit to wear on Christmas Eve.

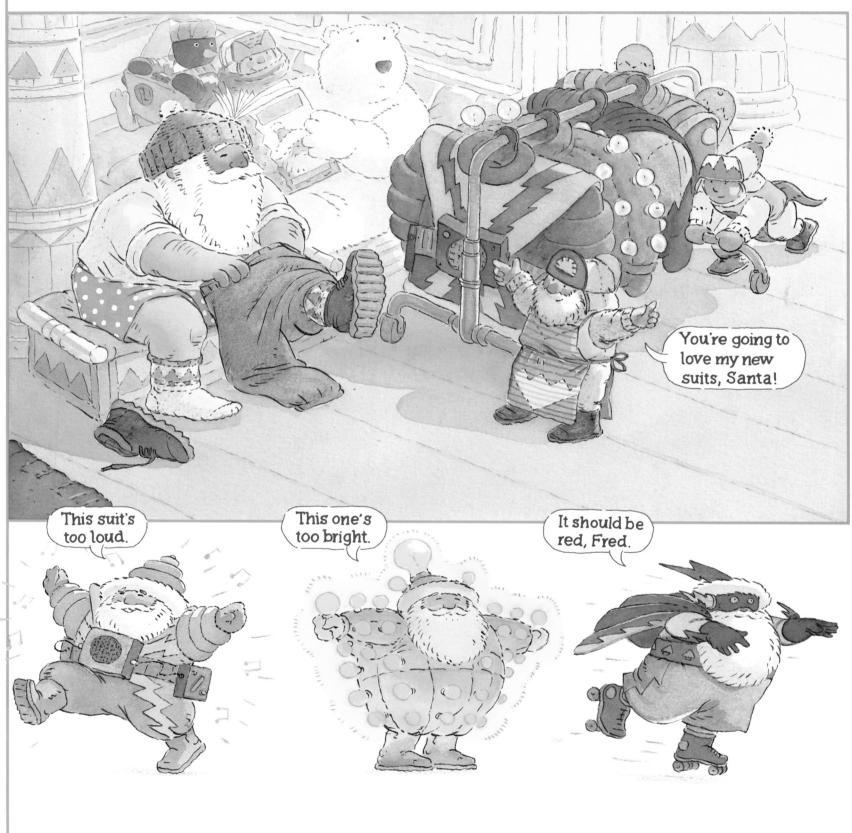

Try my secret rocket suit, Santa.

What happens if I press this button, Fred?

No, stop, Santa!

BOOM

I think this might be better, Santa.

Phew, me too!

Suits me to a tee!

On his way home, Santa drops in to see Pearl and the Knitwits. Clickity, click, clackity, clack. Those Knitwits never stop knitting.

These will keep me nice and warm on Christmas Eve.

The Knitwits have made the snazziest pair of extra-cosy, double-thick, sizzling-yellow long johns you've ever seen. Sid drives us back to the Ice Palace for an early night. Tomorrow — the Reindeer Trials!

SANTA SU

REINDEER TRIALS DAY ON MISTLETOE MOUNTAIN

by chief reporter Percy Penguin in Santa City

It was a crisp and chilly morning, high above Santa City, when one of the most important events of the year took place here yesterday.

Sleigh bells rang all over the North Pole as hundreds of young flying reindeer gathered on Mistletoe Mountain to take part in the Reindeer Trials for a place on Santa's team.

For weeks, Santa's snowmen had been busy building the tricky course that will test the candidates.

SANTA FOLLOWS RACE IN RED BALLOON

At exactly 10 o'clock, wrapped up warmly against the chilly wind, Santa arrived in his red balloon to start the race. Throngs of hopeful reindeer burst through the starting gate and flew off to the first huge hurdle — Chimney Slalom.

Far above them, floating across the clear blue sky, Santa watched the reindeer streak around the course. What a great contest it was. Never before had so many reindeer competed in the Trials.

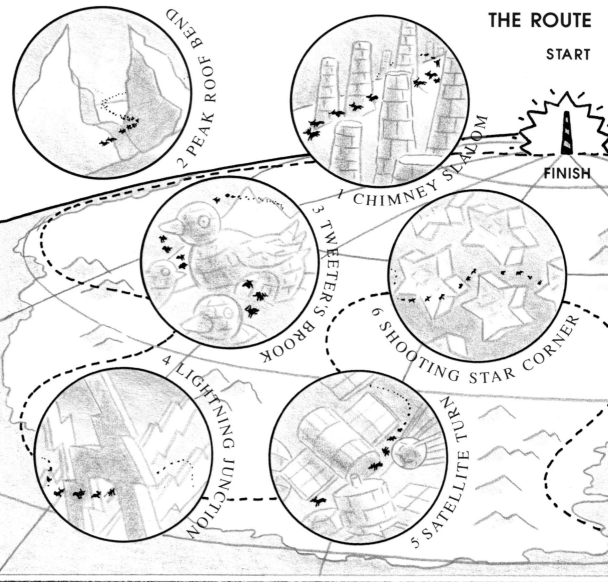

THE ROUTE

START

FINISH

1 CHIMNEY SLALOM

2 PEAK ROOF BEND

3 TWEETER'S BROOK

4 LIGHTNING JUNCTION

5 SATELLITE TURN

6 SHOOTING STAR CORNER

SNOWBALL STOPS PRANCER

It was one of the most difficult courses ever. Only the bravest and best new jumpers made it through Lightning Junction, past Hazard Mountain and through Thunder Pass, the most difficult obstacles in the entire race.

For three hours, Prancer, the favorite, led the way. Then suddenly, as he swooped past Thick Cloud Underpass to Snowball Station, a huge snowball struck him on the head and Ding Dong, Hosanna and Tinsel thundered past.

TINSEL AND DING DONG WIN PLACES ON SANTA'S TEAM

Finally, at the end of an exciting race, the winners, Ding Dong and Tinsel, galloped past the finishing post.

There wasn't an inch between these two magnificent reindeer as they broke the winning tape to the delight of the onlookers.

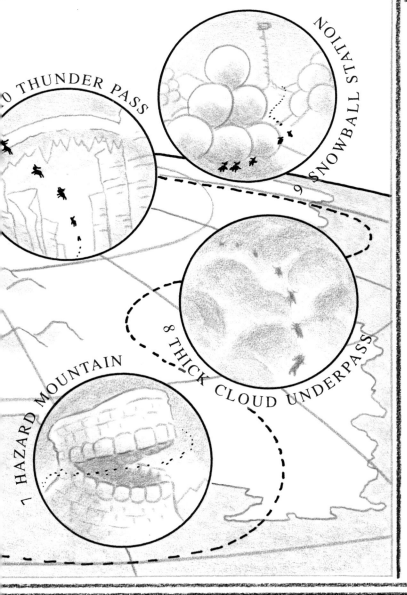

SANTA PRESENTS THE PRIZES

The snowmen roared and the elves cheered loudly as Santa presented the winners with their prizes — special Christmas harnesses with silver bells to wear on the big night.

The Reindeer Trials have ended and the contestants have all gone home. But on Christmas Eve, these two lucky new reindeer will be there, helping to pull Santa's sleigh.

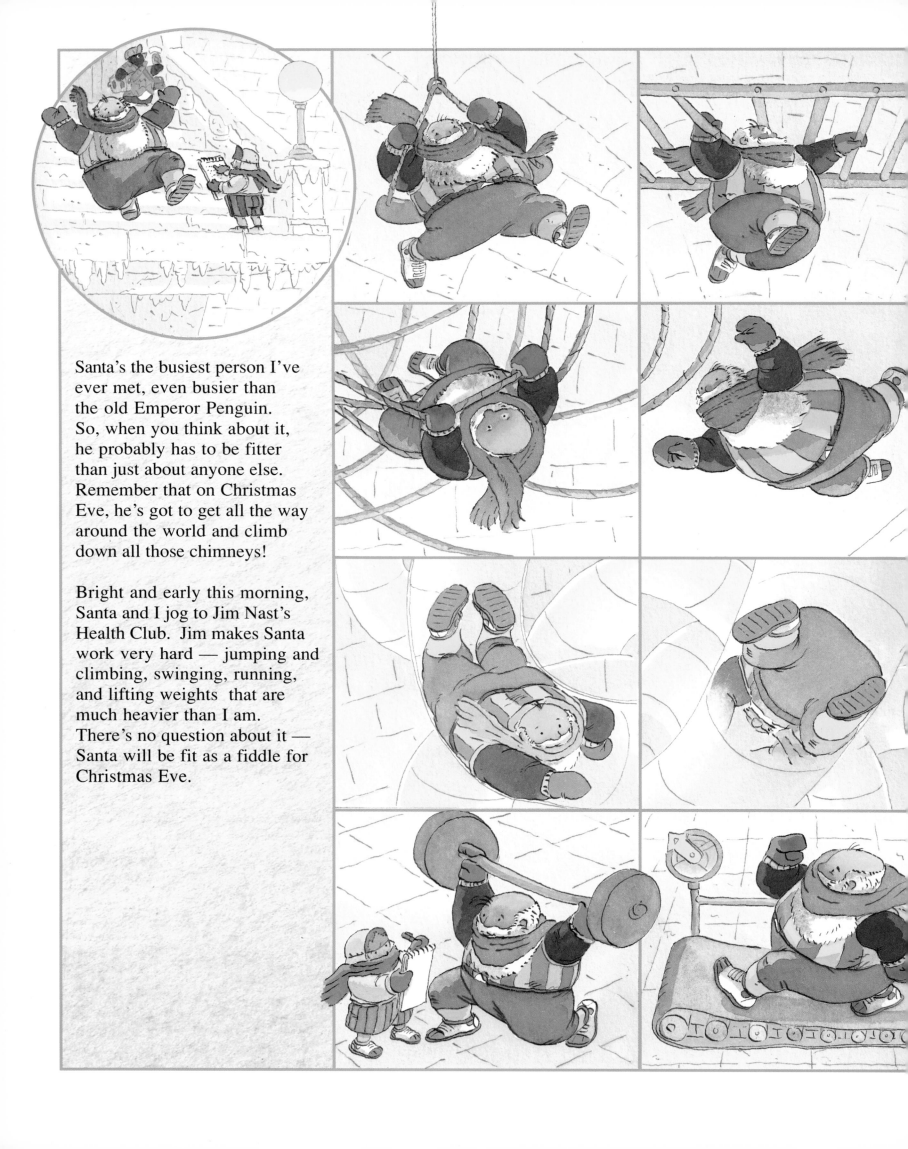

Santa's the busiest person I've ever met, even busier than the old Emperor Penguin. So, when you think about it, he probably has to be fitter than just about anyone else. Remember that on Christmas Eve, he's got to get all the way around the world and climb down all those chimneys!

Bright and early this morning, Santa and I jog to Jim Nast's Health Club. Jim makes Santa work very hard — jumping and climbing, swinging, running, and lifting weights that are much heavier than I am. There's no question about it — Santa will be fit as a fiddle for Christmas Eve.

The next stop is the Santa City School. It's a special school for Santa and the elves. Now what does someone like Santa need to learn, for goodness sake?

For one thing, he's brushing up on his map reading with a clever elf named Compass Rose. Remember, he has to find his way around every single country in the world.

Ali Looyer gives Santa a language lesson to make sure he can read all the signposts on the big night.

Another class is with jolly Miss L. Toe. She teaches Santa how to tiptoe quietly so he won't wake any children while he fills their stockings.

These two little dears aren't doing very well with their sleigh lesson. They can't seem to remember their left from their right. I hope they do better on Christmas Eve.

It's Christmas Eve at last. And Santa's asked *me — yes, me —* Percy Penguin, to go with him on his sleigh. Yippee, what an incredible scoop!

Before we set off, Santa makes his last minute rounds to see that everything's ready for the big night. He checks to see that the reindeer have eaten all their supper. They're going to need lots of carrots to get them through this night!

Next door, Santa's sleigh is given a final inspection. Wow, what a magnificent flying machine!

Ho, ho, ho! I love Christmas so.

Hey, hey, hey! More presents for Santa's sleigh.

The Toy Factory's still buzzing with activity. Those snowmen have been working day and night taking presents to the Sleigh Port. There goes one carrying a huge box of flying penguins!

Ho, ho, ho. It's time for Santa to get dressed.

You're late, Santa.

Good old Gloria. She's got a list of things that Santa needs.

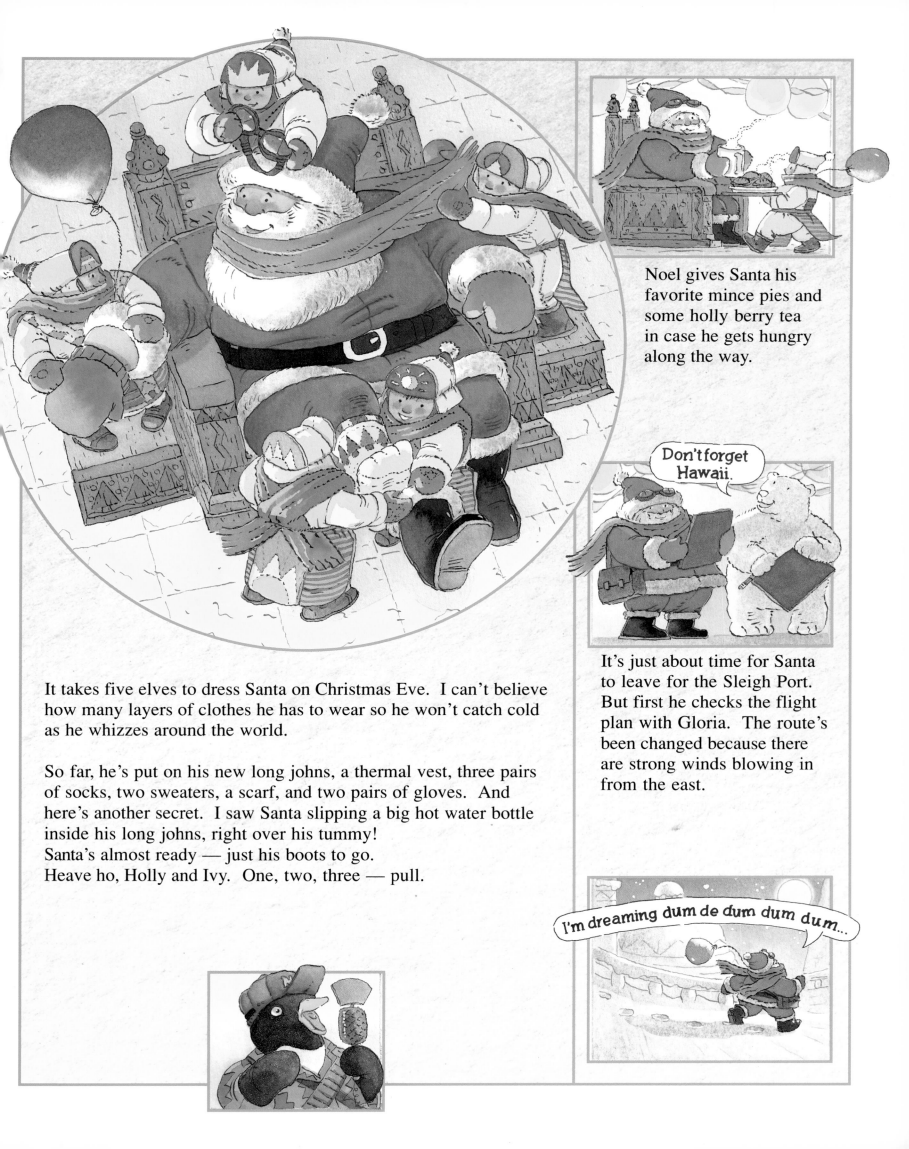

Noel gives Santa his favorite mince pies and some holly berry tea in case he gets hungry along the way.

Don't forget Hawaii.

It's just about time for Santa to leave for the Sleigh Port. But first he checks the flight plan with Gloria. The route's been changed because there are strong winds blowing in from the east.

It takes five elves to dress Santa on Christmas Eve. I can't believe how many layers of clothes he has to wear so he won't catch cold as he whizzes around the world.

So far, he's put on his new long johns, a thermal vest, three pairs of socks, two sweaters, a scarf, and two pairs of gloves. And here's another secret. I saw Santa slipping a big hot water bottle inside his long johns, right over his tummy!
Santa's almost ready — just his boots to go.
Heave ho, Holly and Ivy. One, two, three — pull.

I'm dreaming dum de dum dum dum...

Santa's Sleigh Port is quite out of this world. There are flashing lights, dials and computer screens everywhere.

The whole place is tingling with excitement as Santa and his reindeer get ready to take off.

Santa's helpers are working at a furious pace. The snowmen keep coming with more and more presents. They'll have to hurry. The huge Sleigh Port doors are opening. It's time for Santa to go.

Wait for me, reindeer!

S-s-s-sorry, Frosty.

This is slippery business.

Before we set off, Noel makes sure that all the children are fast asleep.

Robin checks the weather report. Santa will have to watch out for that east wind.

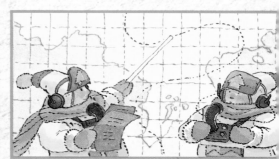

Holly and Ivy give the team of reindeer their final flying instructions.

Everything's ready as Carol guides Santa and the reindeer toward the doors.

Now Gloria jumps out of the sleigh to shout out the final countdown.

Ho, ho, ho, it's time to go. Santa, the reindeer and I are off to fill stockings!

What a take-off. We zoom across the sky faster than a rocket. This is the most exciting night of my life.

One minute we're up in the stars; the next we're diving down, down, down. I never realized before how big the world is. Just think of all the millions of children fast asleep in their beds, dreaming of what Santa might bring them.

You would never believe how much trouble Santa has getting into some houses. Sometimes the chimneys are too small, sometimes they're too big and sometimes there isn't one at all. But Santa never *ever* gives up.

Once he's inside, Santa finds all sorts of other problems as well — big, fierce dogs, hungry cats and very prickly Christmas trees. What a job!

As if that wasn't enough, he sometimes hears children talking. Flapping flippers, don't they know that Santa can't fill stockings until *everybody* is fast asleep.

Santa's got only one more stocking to fill up tonight. Do you know what? It belongs to the little girl who asked him for a flying penguin. What a great surprise she'll have tomorrow morning.

Hurry up, Santa. It's time to fly back to Santa City.

That was fast! We're already back in Santa City. I can see the Ice Palace sparkling in the darkness.

Everyone's come out to welcome us home. Santa's done it again — delivered all his presents without a hitch.

Of course, he couldn't have done it without the reindeer. Everyone agrees they did a wonderful job tonight.

Here comes Gloria. She tells Santa to hurry up and dress for the Christmas party. I wonder what he's going to wear.

Three cheers for Santa!

"Ho, ho, ho!"

Whopping whales! This is the very best party I've ever been to. But all good things must come to an end, and now it's time for me to go home.

Before I leave, I thank Santa for his hospitality, and for letting me in on all his secrets.

I'm going to miss everyone. Goodbye, Santa. Goodbye, elves and snowmen. Goodbye, Santa City. I hope I can come back again one day.